John P. Betker

The M.E. Church and Slavery

Anatiposi

John P. Betker

The M.E. Church and Slavery

Reprint of the original, first published in 1859.

1st Edition 2023 | ISBN: 978-3-38231-272-5

Anatiposi Verlag is an imprint of Outlook Verlagsgesellschaft mbH.

Verlag (Publisher): Outlook Verlag GmbH, Zeilweg 44, 60439 Frankfurt, Deutschland
Vertretungsberechtigt (Authorized to represent): E. Roepke, Zeilweg 44, 60439 Frankfurt, Deutschland
Druck (Print): Books on Demand GmbH, In de Tarpen 42, 22848 Norderstedt, Deutschland

THE

M. E. CHURCH AND SLAVERY,

AS DESCRIBED BY

REVS. H. MATTISON, W. HOSMER, E. BOWEN, D. D.,
D. DE VINNE, AND J. D. LONG,

WITH

A BIBLE VIEW OF THE WHOLE SUBJECT.

BY REV. JOHN P. BETKER.

———◆———

Syracuse, N. Y.:
SAMUEL LEE.
1859.

M. E. CHURCH AND SLAVERY.

The Anti-slavery men in the M. E. Church, occupy a very remarkable position at this time. A position which Christian men cannot occupy and be consistent, if all they say of their Church in her relation to slavery be correct. Their position cannot be defended from the word of God. Nay, rather the word of God plainly condems it.

Contemplating the pictures which they themselves have drawn of the M. E. Church, in her complicity with slavery, no one can, on any scriptural ground, account for these men remaining in her communion another day. In the entire absence of any more favorable light in which to estimate their motives, we are driven to the unpleasant conclusion, that they are governed more by the spirit of sectarianism and love of party in their present operations, than they are by the Spirit of Truth or the Bible. I say not this to give offence. I would not judge these brethren harshly. They, however, have laid themselves liable to such insinuations, or to the equally discreditable one, that the directions given in the Bible in relation to the moral ground they occupy as Christian men, is wholly set aside by them ; and that they have adopted instead thereof, the tricks and traps of political parties as promising greater, and more permanent success than can be hoped for by pursuing the course pointed out in the word of God. Nothing can be plainer than the fact that their position finds no justification in the word of God. Such a position, however specious, is opposed to sound morality, and must, in the end, work evil to all concerned.

In order that this matter may be viewed in its proper light, I shall, present the picture these men have given of the M. E. Church in her connection with Slavery; and compare the picture thus drawn, with the scripture representation of a true and false church.

What do these men say of the M. E. Church in her relation to Slavery?

The Black River Conference of the M. E. Church, at its last session, passed several resolutions in regard to the connection of their Church with Slavery. The preamble and 1st resolution thus read:—

"Whereas, We are most painfully impressed with a sense of the enormity and guilt of slavery as it exists in these United States, and *blush* with *shame* that in the afternoon of the nineteenth century, the Church of God, bears upon her otherwise beautiful visage the plague-spot of slavery, and embraces in her communion slave-holding members, officiaries and ministers;

And Whereas, We believe slave-holding to be a grievous sin against Almighty God, a cruel unmitigated outrage against the enslaved, and in conflict with all that is sacred in divinity and with all that is dear to humanity: therefore,

Resolved, 1st, *That our complicity with this vile abomination places us in the most fearful attitude before the God of holiness and justice*, and our tamness in the cause of human freedom, and slowness to speak for the dumb, call for the deepest humiliation and the most genuine, hearty repentance before God."

This language describes fully the corrupt position of the M. E. Church, in her complicity with the vile abominations of Slavery; but it is not true of the Church of God that she is thus corrupted. The true Church of God, is "the salt of the earth ; " but a church which has become *morally* corrupt, and shown herself to be false to her holy mission on earth, by "embracing in her communion—a grievous sin against Almighty God, (and) a cruel, unmitigated outrage against the enslaved" millions of this land, is thus described in Christ's own words : "If the salt have lost its savour, wherewith shall it be salted ? IT IS THENCEFORTH GOOD FOR NOTHING, BUT TO BE CAST OUT, and to be trodden under foot of men." Mat. v. 13.

The members of the B. R. Conference, in their zeal to prevent secession from their Church, whose wretched corruption causes even them "to blush with shame," nevertheless assume to call her "the Church of God !" But while this assumption may for the time meet the demands of partizans, by preventing secession, it finds no support whatever in the word of God. No Ecclesiastical body that "embraces in its communion slave-holding members, officiaries and ministers," can be scripturally called the Church of God ; and without the sanction of Scripture, every such claim must be false.

The Rev. D. DE VINNE, of the New York East Conference of the M. E. Church, in a pamphlet entitled *The M. E. Church and Slavery*, thus speaks of her present position :

"More than thirty years ago, *we spent the whole of the real anti-slavery capital* our venerated fathers had left us. And at present, notwithstanding our ever, and anon repetition of anti-slaveryism, *the tendency and influence of our Church is for Slavery ;* for its quiet, peaceful continuance in the Church under present circumstances,—THE VERIEST TRADERS IN THE SOULS AND BODIES OF MEN CAN DESIRE NOTHING MORE THAN THIS." Page 87.

In his introduction, he uses this language :

"We deplore the present position of our Church ; and in view of all the ground, having traveled fifteen thousand miles in slave-holding States, and having conversed freely with Methodist slaves and slave-holders, we must here record our solemn and religious testimony, that, in our opinion, *the influence of the M. E. Church, as administered for the last thirty years, has been unfavorable to the emancipation of Slavery, either in our Church, or in our country.*"

Such a Church, to say the least of it, is "salt that has lost its savor, and it is thenceforth good for nothing, but to be cast out, and to be trodden under foot of men."

According to DE VINNE, "the veriest traders in the bodies and souls of men, can desire nothing more" than the present position of the M. E. Church. Christian men have no right, or business to remain in a church that thus makes herself the ally of the basest of men-thieves ! "The law is not made for a righteous man, but for the lawless and disobedient—FOR MEN-STEALERS—and any other thing that is contrary to sound doctrine." 1 Tim. i. 9, 10.

Rev. WM. HOSMER, Editor of the *Northern Independent*, in the No. for June 9th, thus speaks of the M. E. Church :

"It is sad that we have become apostates to freedom,— the toleration among us of a compromising, apologizing, and merely formal opposition to the abomination of Slavery, has depraved the nation. In the M. E. Church,—it is scarcely better."—"The fathers of Methodism were abolitionists of the staunchest kind ; and whatever rules or regulations we have in the Discipline against this sin, have come down to us from them,—we not only have added nothing, but have suffered the rules which they made to become a dead letter."—"The passing by of the Levite on the other side, told the story of his morals, and the *want* of earnest, instant, unyielding devotion to the bondman, tells more explicitly than words could do, the price *we* put upon liberty, and the estimate *we* form of the wrong done to the innocent man who is converted into a chattel. While we are thus ambiguous, touching this *boundless robbery*, A PROFESSION OF CHRISTIANITY AVAILS US NOTHING. No skill, no solemnity, no earnestness, no profession, can possibly unite sin and holiness, slavery and religion."

The M. E. Church and Slavery are united, and therefore she is not the embodiment of the religion of Christ; in other words she is not a Church of Christ, " her profession of Christianity avails nothing ;" her claim must be false. It is just as reasonable to suppose that a professor of religion who has become an apostate, is still a genuine Christian, as to suppose that a church which becomes apostate to the common rights of humanity, is still a Church of Christ.

Rev. J. D. LONG, of the Philadelphia Conference of the M. E. Church, thus describes the M. E. Church in his work, entitled, *Pictures of Slavery.* After having shown the high anti-slavery ground occupied by the fathers of Methodism, he says :

" We have painfully to admit that the Church did after-wards *fall from her noble and New Testament position* on the subject of Slavery ; and many of those fathers tried to undo *with their own hands*, what they had so nobly accomplished. So that in 1808, was stricken out of the Discipline, all that related to private members—private members could hold for life, their fellow-creatures, in bondage—give them away to their children during their life time—and leave them in perpetual slavery. *So the whole ground was in effect conceded to Slavery.* What a fearful history the M. E. Church has to read to the world by this concession ! A HISTORY WRITTEN WITH THE BLOOD AND TEARS OF OPPRESSED THOUSANDS ! Private members holding slaves, soon involved class-leaders, exhorters, local preachers, and traveling preachers, and finally *debauched the moral sentiment of the whole Church."* Pictures, p. 30, 31.

A church, whose "history is written in the blood and tears of oppressed thousands,"—whose "whole moral sentiment has become debauched," ceases at once to be the Church of Christ, whatever may have been her character before she became thus polluted. Of such a church, it may be said in the language of Jeremiah : " In thy skirts is found the blood of the souls of the poor innocents ; I have not found it by secret search, but upon all these. Behold I will plead with thee because thou sayest. I have not sinned. Why gaddest thou about so much to change thy way? The Lord hath rejected thy confidences, and thou shalt not prosper in them." (Jer. ii. 34, 37.) " Come out of her my people, that ye be not partakers of her sins, and that ye receive not of her plagues." Rev. xviii. 4.

On pages 34, 35, he thus graphically portrays the present position of the M. E. Church :

" *We have a pro-slavery Discipline,* which allows our private members in DELAWARE, MARYLAND, and VIRGINIA to hold for gain, to give away, and transmit by will to their heirs, as chattels personal, *souls for whom Christ died.* The slave can be sold for their debts at any time. They can give them away to relatives, who can sell them to the negro-buyers at pleasure ; *and do all this according to the discipline of the Church ;* AND THEY CANNOT BE EXPELLED FOR IT."

A church whose members can thus traffic in the souls for whom Christ died, "and do this according to the Discipline of the Church," cannot be the Church of Christ. The idea is preposterous that Christ would own a Church as his whose very Discipline ignores the great purposes of his mission to our earth. That mission he thus describes, "The Spirit of the Lord is upon me, because he hath anointed me *to preach the Gospel to the poor*, he hath sent me to heal the broken-hearted, *to preach deliverance to the captives*, and recovering of sight to the blind, TO SET AT LIBERTY THEM THAT ARE BRUISED." Luke iv. 18.

Bro. LONG goes on farther to say :

" I make bold to declare that there are more slaves owned *now* by members of the M. E. Church than in 1845. ' Why you astonish me !' Says one, ' I thought that anti-slavery principles were on the increase, since the division of the Church.' But the fact is, our members don't care one cent how much the preachers slap each other and the bishops about holding slaves ; nor how much they talk about slavery in the abstract and advocate colonization, if they but abuse abolitionists without defining the term, and never hint, even in private conversation, that it is a sin in private members to hold slaves, and get rich upon their labor. When you strike that key-note, you will find out that *there is very little difference between the laity of the M. E. Church North and the laity of the M. E. Church South, IN THEORY OR PRACTICE ON THE SUBJECT OF SLAVERY.* Do the members of the Church South hold slaves for life? So do *ours.* Do *their* slaves live in promiscuous intercourse ? So do *ours.*"

On page 288, he says further on this point :

" The M. E. Church South charge the laity of our Church with *mercenary* slave-holding ; and, as an honest man, I must say that *the charge is true to the* VERY LETTER."

On page 49, he says :

" I cannot speak for the Baltimore Conference, though it is certain it has a vastly larger slave-holding territory than the Philadelphia Conference. If that Conference has jurisdiction over one thousand slave-holders, and these own 3000 slaves, *then we have* 6000 *slaves owned by* 2000 *members of the M. E. Church,* ALL SHELTERED BY THE DISCIPLINE OF OUR CHURCH."

Here are facts and figures from an accredited minister of the M. E. Church, which it would be well for our people to remember. They fully corroborate the charges we have made against the M. E. Church for years past. A Church, whose Discipline shelters her members in this wholesale bartering in the God-given rights of our fellow-beings, cannot be the Church of God! The following Scriptures more properly apply to such a Church:

"Wo unto them that decree unrighteous decrees, (Pro-slavery Disciplines for instance,) and that write grievous-ness which they have prescribed; to turn aside the needy from judgment, and take away the right of the poor of my people, that widows may be their prey, and that they may rob the fatherless. And what will ye do in the day of visita-tion, and in the desolation which shall come from far? To whom will ye flee for help? And where will ye leave your glory?" Isaiah x. 1–3. "Hear ye this, O, ye that swallow up the needy, even to make the poor of the land to fail. *That buy the poor for silver, and the needy for a pair of shoes;* the Lord hath sworn by the excellency of Jacob, *surely I will never forget any of their works.*" Amos viii. 4–7.

"I will be a swift witness against those *that oppress the hireling in his wages,* the widow and the fatherless, *and that turn aside the stranger from his right* and fear not me, saith the Lord of hosts." Mat. iii. 5.

"As a cage is full of birds, so are their houses full of deceit: therefore they are become great, and waxen rich. They are waxen fat, they shine: yea, they over-pass the deeds of the wicked; they judge not the cause, the cause of the fatherless, yet they prosper; and the right of the needy do they not judge. Shall I not visit for these things? saith the Lord; shall not my soul be avenged on such a nation?" Jer. v. 27–29. "Wo unto you, scribes and pharisees, hypocrites! for ye devour widows' houses, and for a pretence make long prayer; therefore ye shall receive the greater damnation. Wo unto you, scribes and pharisees, hypocrites! for ye pay tithe of mint, and anise, and cum-min, and have omitted the weightier matters of the law, judgment, mercy and faith: these ought ye to have done, and not leave the other undone. Ye blind guides, which strain at a gnat, and swallow a camel. Wo unto you, scribes and pharisees, hypocrites! for ye are like unto whited sepulchres, which indeed appear beautiful outward, but are within full of dead men's bones, and all uncleanness. Even so ye also outwardly appear righteous unto men, but within ye are full of hypocrisy and iniquity." Math. xxiii.

These are a few of the dreadful words God has spoken against those associations that "shelter" "the theory and practice" of the "sum of all villainies" among them. These dreadful words cannot apply to the true Church of God. Therefore, those churches to whom they do apply are not the true churches of Jesus Christ. They properly apply to the M. E. Church, if Rev. J. D. Long has correctly portrayed her present position on the slavery question, and therefore her claim to be a Church of Christ is inadmissible.

" Wherefore come out from among them, and be ye separate said the Lord." 2 Cor. vi. 17.

The Rev. H. Mattison, in his *Impending Crisis*, thus describes and characterizes the pro-slavery position of the M. E. Church:

" In the M. E. Church *proper*, we have now some 15,000 slave-holders, holding 100,000 slaves; with slave-holding leaders, stewards, trustees, and local preachers, by hundreds, if not by thousands. It has also entered the traveling ministry, and slave-holders are openly tolerated in several of the Conferences, *without the slightest disapprobation*. Members of our churches in New York, and Philadelphia, if not in Central New York, own slaves in Maryland and Virginia." Page 117.

" *We are now as a Church more deeply and criminally involved in slave-holding than at any former period of our history.*" Page 41. " We have now from ten to twenty thousand slave-holders in our church; among whom are *hundreds of leaders, stewards, and local preachers, deacons and elders,* WHO OWN, RAISE, BUY AND SELL SLAVES, as suits their convenience and interest, and with utter impunity. THERE CANNOT BE LESS THAN ONE HUNDRED THOUSAND SLAVES NOW OWNED, AND HELD IN BONDAGE BY METHODISTS, IN THE NORTHERN PORTION OF THE ORIGINAL METHODIST EPISCOPAL CHURCH,—and *no efforts are made on the part of the executive authorities of the Church to stay this incoming tide of sin and corruption.* Now if any man can look these facts in the face, and not say that we are infinitely worse off, so far as connection with slavery is concerned, than we were before the division of 1844, we envy him not his knowledge, or judgment, or candor. Much as it may mortify our denominational pride, we may better own the whole truth, and by God's help seek to recover ourselves out of *the snare of the devil,* than to conceal, or refuse to look at the truth, till it is too late to retrieve our lost character, and moral power. So far as this subject is concerned, THE M. E. CHURCH IN AMERICA IS A FALLEN CHURCH. Bating what genuine anti-slavery principle there is in the Northern Conferences, from the crown of the head to the soles of the feet, there is no soundness in us, but wounds, and bruises, and putrefying sores ; that have not been bound up, neither mollified with ointment. And our condition in this respect is growing worse and worse, every year, and every day." Pages 84, 85.

"*Thus we stand to this day* AS A DENOMINATION, AMONG THE ABETTORS AND UPHOLDERS OF SLAVERY." Page 109.

No one can compare this description Bro. MATTISON gives of the M. E. Church, with the Bible description of the Church of God, and not be struck with the fact that her claim to be the Church of God finds no support whatever in the Bible. As proof of the truth of this statement, instance the following points of comparison :

1st. Bro. Mattison says of the connection of the M. E. Church with the "sum of all villainies," "From the crown of the head to the soles of the feet *there is no soundness in us.*" Compare this picture by the one drawn by St. Paul of the Church of Christ. " Christ also loved the Church, and gave himself for it, that he might present it to himself a glorious church, *not having spot or wrinkle*, OR ANY SUCH THING ; but that it should be holy and WITHOUT BLEMISH." Ephes. v. 25–27. The church which Paul describes is "*without blemish.*" The church which MATTISON describes *has " no soundness in"* her. The church, therefore, that MATTISON describes is not the Church of Christ.

2d. Bro. MATTISON says of the corrupt state of the M. E. Church, in her connection with slavery : " Our condition in this respect *is growing worse and worse*, every year, and every day." St. Paul, describing " the household of God," says it is "built upon the foundation of the apostles and prophets, Jesus Christ himself being the chief corner stone, in whom all the building fitly framed together, *groweth unto a holy temple* in the Lord." Ephes. ii. 19, 21. The church which Paul describes " *groweth unto a holy temple.*" The church which MATTISON describes, is "*growing worse and worse,*" in the pollutions of slavery. MATTISON'S church, therefore, is not the church that Paul describes ; and consequently is not the Church of Christ.

3d. Bro. MATTISON says of the M. E. Church : " We stand this day *as a denomination among the abettors and upholders of slavery.*" St. Paul says, " The *church of the living God (is) the pillar and ground of truth.*" 1 Tim iii. 15. This remarkable difference between the church which Paul describes and the one MATTISON describes, renders the claim of the latter, to be the church that Paul speaks of, absurd and ridiculous.

4th. Bro. MATTISON represents the M. E. Church as being in the " *snare of the devil ;*" and on page 85, (see Crisis) speaking of the utter pro-slaveryism of the M. E. Church South, he says, "in the Northern portion *we are hastening on to the same consummation,* so far as our slave territory is concern d, *as fast as time, and the powers of darkness can hurry us to ruin."* Our Lord Jesus Christ thus speaks of his own church : "Upon this rock I will build my church, and *the gates of hell (the powers of darkness) shall not prevail against it."* Mat. xvi. 18.

MATTISON's church is "*in the snare of the devil,—and the powers of darkness are hurrying her to ruin,"* and consequently the gates of hell have prevailed against his church ; therefore, his church is not the Church of Christ, for the gates of hell shall not prevail against the Church of Christ. "And unto the angel of the church in Smyrna, write : these things saith the first and the last— I know thy works, and tribulations, and poverty, (but thou art rich,) and I *know the blasphemy of them which say they are Jews, and are not, but are the synagogue of Satan."* Rev. ii. 8, 9.

"What concord hath Christ with Belial? or what part hath he that believeth with an infidel? And what agreement hath the temple of God with idols?—Wherefore, come out from among them and be ye separate saith the Lord." 2 Cor. vi. 15–17.

ELIAS BOWEN, D. D., a member of the Oneida Conference of the M. E. Church, has recently written a book, entitled *Slavery in the M. E. Church.* From this work I will quote a few faithfully drawn pictures of the M. E. Church, in her complicity with "the sum of all villainies." On the 4th page of his introduction, he thus speaks :

"The *demon of slavery* which entered into the Methodist societies at an early day, and which *our fathers crim-*

inally failed to cast out of the church at the time of her organization, has at length become *installed over us as the* GENIUS LOCI of our institutions and government ; and all our administrations and movements *are now subject to the domineering surveillance of this* RUTHLESS DIVINITY."

Let the reader compare this state of things in the M. E. Church, with the following view of the true Church of Christ given by St. Paul : "The God of our Lord Jesus Christ, the Father of glory, hath put all things under his feet, and gave him to be head over all things to the church, which is his body." Ephes. i. 17, 22, 23.

"The demon of slavery" is the presiding divinity of Dr. BOWEN's church ; but the Lord Jesus Christ is the presiding Divinity of the church which St. Paul speaks of, therefore, Dr. BOWEN's church is not a Church of Christ. Christ, and the "demon of slavery" cannot be presiding divinities in the same church, for "what concord hath Christ with Belial?" (2 Cor. vi.) Where may we look for "the synagogue of Satan" if not in the M. E. Church, whose presiding genius is the "demon of slavery ?"

Again, the Dr. says :

"For some time previous to the last General Conference, the church had been deeply convinced of the great evil of slavery. But since that time, like an awakened sinner, who has shaken off his convictions, by resisting the influences of the Spirit, she has lost all sense of the guilt of holding her fellow-creatures in bondage, and relapsed into a state of profoundest apathy. *She has taken the viper into her bosom,* and according to the teachings of *the last General Conference, and most of our editors,* it would be a violation of the constitution of the church to cast it out! *And yet she refuses to alter the constitution!"* Pages 11–13.

A church whose constitution would be violated if slavery, "the vilest sin that ever saw the sun," was cast out of her bosom, cannot possibly be the Church of Christ. A section of the constitution of the true Church of Christ thus reads, " I wrote unto you in an epistle, not to company with fornicators ; yet not altogether the fornicators of this world, or with the covetous, or EXTORTIONERS, or with idolaters, for then must ye needs go out of the world. But now I have written unto you not to keep company, if any man that is called a brother be a fornicator, or COVE-TOUS, or an idolater, or a railer, or a drunkard, OR AN EXTORTIONER, with such an one no not to eat." 1 Cor. v. 9, 11. "I would not that ye should have fellowship with devils." 1 Cor. x. 20. The constitution of Christ's true church would be violated if " the sum of all villainies" were admitted to her fellowship ; but the constitution of the M. E. Church admits " the sum of all villainies" to her very bosom ; nay, she would violate her constitution were she to cast this viper out of her bosom ! Christ's Church, and the M. E. Church, therefore, are not identical, for they have not the same head, nor the same constitution. For if Dr. Bowen has justly represented the M. E. Church, " the demon of slavery is the *genius loci* of her institutions and government," and a pro-slavery Discipline is her constitution. While Jesus Christ is the head, and the word of God is the constitution of the Church of Christ.

I will now give Dr. Bowen's definition of Slavery, together with extracts from his book showing the pro-slavery character of the M. E. Church. The Dr. thus expresses himself in regard to slavery :

" If we have spoken of the enormous sin of Slavery in strong and decided terms, or denounced it as *a crime of the deepest die—an exhibition of depravity which it were shocking to contemplate in the most uncivilized and barbarous state of society even.—*we ask no man's pardon. Our conceptions of *the unparalleled wickedness of Slavery,* and the abhorrence with which we regard an evil so gigantic and appalling in its character, have utterly failed, through the feebleness of language, to manifest their full strength and vigor, or to give adequate expression of their intensity. When Wesley said of Slavery, 'it is the sum of all villainies,' *he fell below the reality.* IT IS PLUS ALL THAT IN ITS MILDEST FORM ; and all the Buchanans and Taneys this side of hell can make nothing less of it. *We might look in vain for the entire aggregation, or absolute embodiment of crimes of all sorts and descriptions in any other single institution on earth.* The annals of the darkest period of the dark ages, *when* slave-holding was prevalent in most parts of the world, and Rome and *Romanism stood pre-eminent in the history of crime ; even the annals of that period furnish no parallel in wickedness and cruelty to American Slavery!"* Pages 120, 121.

Now how does the M. E. Church stand in relation to " this unparalleled wickedness," " this aggregation of all sorts and descriptions of crimes ?" The Doctor furnishes us with a very plain and distinct answer to this inquiry. Here it is :

"The institution of Slavery being *practically sustained by her*, and the *shield* of her Discipline, of her administration, and of her ruling authorities *being thrown around it,* SHE IS TO ALL IN I ENTS AND PURPOSES A PRO-SLAVERY CHURCH. Her Discipline is pro-slavery, since it provides by statutory enactment for the existence of slavery, and regulates and upholds it. Her administration is pro-slavery. for it admits slave-holders to her communion, keeps them in her communion, and protects them in all the rights and privileges of membership, the occupancy of the sacred office not excepted. And her ruling authorities are pro-slavery. And what more is necessary to constitute her pro-slavery ? *Surely nothing but the name.* We contend that the M. E. Church is a pro-slavery church, and it is vain for her to pretend to the contrary. As well might she maintain that the drunkard, the adulterer, or the highway robber, is opposed to the practice he pursues, as that the church is opposed to slavery, while she continues to hold slaves. And as she has no right to assume the character, so neither has she any right to bear the name of an anti-slavery church. It is by this *bold dissimulation*—THIS SACRELIGIOUS FORGERY of the name of a class of men she despises in her heart—that she continues to *keep up a reputation for humanity*, and enables herself the more effectually to carry on her crusade against the anti-slavery cause." Pages 52, 53.

I beg the reader to remember that this is not the language of such infidels as STEPHEN S. FOSTER, who wrote " The Brotherhood of Thieves." but that it is the language of ELIAS BOWEN, a Doctor of Divinity, of the M. E. Church, one who is so warmly attached to the M. E. Church that he very tenderly and affectionately calls her his mother! And such a mother! May heaven save the world from her nursing!

A church " that practically sustains a crime of the deepest die," an unparalleled wickedness," the " absolute embodiment of crimes of all sorts and descriptions"—one that " is to all intents and purposes a pro-slavery church," and that deliberately, and ' boldly dissimulates" her true character, and commits a " sacreligious forgery" that she may the more successfully uphold and defend man-stealing and men-thieves " in her crusade against the anti-slavery cause," is additionally guilty of a most blasphemous falsehood, when she calls herself the church of the kind, the good, the holy and ever-blessed Saviour! The audacity of the claim of the M. E. Church to be the Church of God, in view of the picture given by Dr. BOWEN of her complicity with " the sum of all villainies," is scarcely surpassed by the brazened faced wickedness of Slavery itself! A pro-slavery church is a combination of moral forces arrayed against the best interests of humanity! A pro-slavery church is the most formidable obstacle in the way of the ultimate triumphs of the Gospel of the blessed God! A pro-slavery church is the strongest arm of power on the side of the oppressors of this land! A pro-slavery church is the altar of sacrifice upon which millions of human souls are immolated to the atrocious demon of American Slavery! God is dishonored! Christianity is burlesqued! and common sense is outraged, when we call a pro-slavery church the Church of the living God! How emphatically do the following Scriptures apply to the M. E. Church as portrayed by Dr. BOWEN:

"There is a conspiracy of her prophets in the midst thereof, like a roaring lion ravening the prey; they have devoured souls,—her priests have violated my law, and have profaned my holy things; they have put no difference between the holy and profane,—I am profaned among them. Her princes in the midst thereof are like wolves ravening the prey, to shed blood, *and to destroy souls, to get dishonest gain.* Her prophets have daubed them with untempered mortar, seeing vanity, *and devining lies unto them.* The people of the land have used oppression, and exercised robbery, and have vexed the poor and needy." Ezel. xxii. 25–29. "Ye are of your father the devil, and the lusts of your father ye will do, he was a murderer from the beginning, and abode not in the truth, because there is no truth in him. When he speaketh a lie, he speaketh of his own, for he is a liar, and the father of it." John viii. 44. "YE ARE FORGERS OF LIES! *Ye are all physicians of no value.*" Job xiii. 4. "Beware of false prophets which come to you in sheep's clothing. *but inwardly they are ravening wolves.*" Math. vii. 15. "Such are false prophets, *deceitful workers, transforming themselves into apostles of Christ.* And no marvel, for Satan himself is transformed into an angel of light. Therefore it is no great thing, if his ministers be also transformed as ministers of righteousness, whose end shall be according to their works." 2 Cor. xi. 13–15. "Be not ye therefore partakers with them—have no fellowship with the unfruitful works of darkness, but rather reprove them." Ephes. v. 7, 11.

Here is another faithfully drawn picture of the present position of the M. E. Church from the pen of Dr. Bowen. The picture will speak for itself:

"The slave, having been out-lawed by the State, and adjuged to 'possess no rights' which a white man is bound to respect, turns to the church for sympathy and protection; but is told that no protection can be afforded him by her. It is in vain he pleads the design of Christian discipline, and the duty of the church to exercise it for the redress of the aggrieved, and the punishment of the aggressor. Here, too, he finds himself an out-law ; the church having adopted the civil law as the rule of her conduct in relation to slavery, *and conspired with the State to enslave him.* The church, which was designed to be an asylum for the oppressed, has become an asylum for the oppressor ! The hunted, panting lamb is pursued by the devouring wolf even into the sheep-fold, and there's no protection ! He is hunted, and worried, and devoured under the very eye of the shepherd, and there's no protection! Nay, the shepherd himself becomes the devouring wolf, feeding and fatting and rioting upon the blood of his hopeless victim, and there's no protection ! And can it be that this devilish policy is upheld and practiced by the church—that she recognizes no right of the slave which she is bound to respect ? Aye, we are sorry to say it, but it is even so ! *All this is sanctioned, and practiced and baptized as an institution of humanity and benevolence, by the church."* Pages 35, 36.

Let the reader remember that Dr. Bowen, who presents this horrible picture of the M. E. Church to the world. is a member of the Oneida Conference of the M. E. Church in good and regular standing. And let it also be remembered that he is a Doctor of Divinity of the M. E. Church and must therefore be supposed to have represented the true state of his church. Associations upholding and practicing " this Devilish policy," as the Doctor terms it, are thus denounced in God's word :

" Here this word, ye kine of Bashan, that are in the mountains of Samaria, which *oppress the poor, and crush the needy, which say to their masters, bring, and let us drink.* The Lord hath sworn by his holiness, that lo, the day shall come upon you, that he will take you away with hooks, and your posterity with fish-hooks." Amos iv. 1, 2.. " *Forasmuch, therefore, as your treading is upon the poor, and ye take from him burdens of wheat:* ye have built houses of hewn stones, but ye shall not dwell in them ; ye have planted pleasant vineyards, but ye shall not drink wine of them. *For I know your mighty sins ; they afflict the just, they take a bribe, and they turn aside the poor in the gate from their right.* I hate, I despise your feasts-days, and I will not smell in your solemn assemblies. Though ye offer me burnt offerings, and your peace offerings I will not accept them. Take thou away from me the noise of thy songs ; for I will not hear the melody of thy viols." Amos v. 11, 12, 21, 22, 23.

How palpable, in their application, are these words to the M. E. Church, as portrayed above by Dr. Bowen? The people whom the prophet addressed were once God's people, but they degenerated into oppression and injustice ; and " forasmuch as their treading was upon the poor—and they turned aside the poor in the gate (the place where justice was administered) from their right ;" God rejected them and refused to acknowledge them in their most solemn religious services, and sent them, finally, into captivity. If God be unchangeable, he must for the same reasons reject and disown the M. E. Church as his people, for she has ceased to be the asylum of the oppressed, and " has become the asylum of the oppressor." The slave flees in vain to her gates for protection, for she has " conspired with the State to enslave him. He is hunted, and worried and devoured under the very eye of the shepherd.

Nay, the shepherd himself becomes the devouring wolf, feeding, and fatting and rioting upon the blood of his hopeless victim!"

" Pilate and Herod friends!
Chief priests and rulers, as of old combined!
Just God and holy! is that Church which lends
Strength to the Spoiler, Thine?

Woe! woe! to all who grind
Their brethren of a common Father down!
To all who plunder from the Immortal Mind
Its bright and glorious crown!

Woe to the Priesthood! Woe
To those whose hire is with the price of blood!
Perverting, darkening, changing, as they go,
The searching truths of God.

Their glory and their might
Shall perish! And their names shall be
Vile before all the people, in the light
Of a world's Liberty."

In the following extracts from Dr. Bowen's work, we are led to contemplate the motives influencing the M. E. Church in her present connection with Slavery. On pages 141, 142. the Doctor says:

"What shall we say for the M. E. Church in relation to this awful subject? Why, that she has gone in for slavery, *ostensibly* for the *legal relation*, which she *pretends* to maintain for the good of the slave, *but practically, and to all intents and purposes for the* WHOLE SLAVE SYSTEM, WITH ALL ITS ABOMINATIONS AND CRUELTIES. 'O tell it not in Gath, publish it not in the streets of Askelon,'—that this church *practically endorses* a despotism, *the vilest, the most cruel, and the most fiendish this side of hell, by receiving it into her bosom, and extending over it the ægis of her administration and discipline.*"

But says the Doctor, speaking of the legal relation of Slavery:

"To cure or reform slavery, is to destroy it, by destroying the legal relation on which it depends for its existence. This everybody knows. The slave-holder knows it. The church knows it. She knows that slavery and the legal relation stand or fall together ; and it is because of her interest in 'the peculiar institution,' and her determination to uphold it—*cruelties and all*—for the benefits she expects to derive from it, that she hugs the legal relations with so much tenacity. 'It is by this craft she has her wealth,' and the love of gain having eaten out her spirituality and her conscience, she must be expected to cry, 'Great is Diana of the Ephesians.'" Page 110.

Reader, look at this black picture! It is drawn by a master hand—a Doctor of Divinity. This is a portrait of his own church—it is, therefore, reasonable to suppose that he would not represent her character worse than it really is. Look, I say, at this picture! A church without spirituality !—without a conscience ! These having been eaten out by the love of gain !—a gain derived from "practically endorsing a despotism, the vilest ! the most cruel ! and the most fiendish this side of hell !! A church "that goes in for the whole slave system with all its abominations and cruelties !" A church fixed in "her determination to up' hold this system—cruelties and all—for the benefit she expects to derive from it !" For "by this craft she has her wealth !" A church that does these things cannot be a Church of Christ ! Where, in all God's holy book, can one passage be found proving such a church to be the Church of God ? We search in vain for the text ! But every here and there, as we turn over the sacred pages, we meet with passages all aglow with the quenchless wrath of Jehovah, when a foul mass of moral corruption like the M. E. Church, as portrayed by Dr. Bowen, crawls into the light of Divine revelation. Here are a few such passages : "Thus saith the Holy One of Isreal, because ye despise this word, and *trust in oppression* and *perverseness, and stay thereon*. Therefore this iniquity shall be to you as a breach ready to fall, swelling out in a high wall, *whose breaking cometh suddenly at an instant.*" Is. xxx. 12, 13. " *Thine eyes and thine heart are not but for thy covetousness*, and for to shed innocent blood, *and for oppression, and for violence to do it.* Therefore thus saith the Lord, concerning Jehoiakim, the son of Josiah, king of Judah. He shall be buried with the burial of an ass, drawn and cast forth beyond the gates of Jerusalem." Jer. xxii. 17, 19. (That is outside of the pales of God's true church.) " Thou hast taken usury and increase, and thou has greedily gained of thy neighbors by extortion, and hast forgotten me saith the Lord God. *Behold therefore I have smitten mine hand at thy dishonest gain which thou hast made.* Thou wast perfect in thy ways from the day thou wast created, *till iniquity was found in thee.* By the multitude of thy merchandise they have filled thee with violence, and thou has sinned. Therefore I will cast thee as profane out of the mountain of God, (that is out of the true Church of God,) and I will destroy thee." Ezel. xxviii. 15, 16.

" Were they ashamed *when they had committed abomination?* Nay, they were not at all ashamed, neither could they blush (conscience being eaten out ;) *therefore they shall fall among them that fall;* at the time I visit them they shall be cast down, saith the Lord." Jer. vi. 15.

" Thus saith the Lord ; for three transgressions of Israel, and for four, I will not turn away the punishment thereof, because they sold the *righteous for silver, and the poor for a pair of shoes.* That pant after the dust of the earth on the head of the poor." Amos ii. 6, 7. " Know ye not that the unrighteous shall not inherit the Kingdom of God ? Be not deceived ; neither fornicators, nor idolaters, nor adulterers, nor effeminate, nor abusers of themselves with mankind, nor thieves, nor covetous, nor drunkards, nor revilers, nor extortioners, shall inherit the Kingdom of God." 1 Cor. vi. 9, 10.

Not a sentence in all these fearful denunciations of God have the remotest application to the true Church of Christ. But they have a peculiar force and significancy when applied to the M. E. Church as she is described by Dr. Bowen, and if the Doctor has given a true representation of the M. E. Church, she cannot be the Church of God. "Come out of her, my people, that ye be not partakers of her sins, and that ye receive not of her plagues." Rev. xviii. 4.

Are there any hopes entertained by intelligent anti. slavery men in the M. E. Church that she will change her position on the question of Slavery? If such hopes be entertained, and if there be sufficient grounds for such hopes, then whatever may be said of the back-slidden state of. the M. E. Church on the great question of human freedom, she may be restored to her place and station in the Divine favor. Dr. Bowen is perhaps as well, if not better, qualified to give us the best possible information on this point. The following quotations are from his work :

"Slavery was never so deeply rooted in the M. E. Church—never so bold and defiant—as at the present juncture. Slavery has taken hold of the vitals of the church ;—we have already reached a fearful crisis in the history of our church." Pages 160, 161. "We fear that the church will continue to practice an abomination in which she *has become too thoroughly steeped* to have much sense of *her wickedness*, or to forbear to justify it by such pretexts and apologies as shall be calculated to allay any *qualms of conscience that still may linger in her bosom*, and ward off the blow of admonition and warning *so justly aimed at her by the friends of God and humanity.*"

Page 86. "The Jewish Church, abandoned of God, and the cup of her iniquity full, *imagined herself invincible*; and when at the point of ruin, the wrath of an insulted Heaven lowering over her guilty head, and signs portentious of her approaching overthrow fast gathering around her; she still felt secure and confidently looked for deliverance from the perils of a besieging army till her walls were battered down, her temple was wrapped in flames, and the streets of her metropolis flowed in blood! In like manner the Church of Rome *having lost all the nature and spirit of true religion*, and degenerated into the character and condition of anti-Christ—the mother of harlots—the whore of Babylon—had reached a point of *advancement* which seemed to her to suggest and authorize the claim of *infallibility!* And what marvel is it that the M. E. Church should claim to be anti-slavery,—at the very time she is yielding herself up to the control of the slave power. She has pursued her wicked oppressions of the black man till she has become too blind to see, and too hard to feel, or acknowledge the absurdity of claiming to be anti-slavery, while holding her fellow-creatures in bondage. In laboring to deceive others, she has been left, by an awful retribution, to deceive herself. How surely does she 'put light for darkness, and darkness for light; calling evil good, and good evil.' And who wonders that a church that can cherish the blinding, corrupting, and damning sin of Slavery in her bosom, should come to substitute her growing numbers, her multiplied and costly temples, her popularity and influence for the genuine scriptural evidences of evangelical piety?" Pages 145, 146. "This dreadful cancer (Slavery) was upon the face ecclesiastic at our first organization. And it has continued to spread and rage and rankle till it has eaten into her very vitals, diffusing its moral virus over the whole system! But she heeds it not! She seems not to be aware of her condition! She has sinned so long and against so much light and knowledge, that she appears to be 'given over to hardness of heart, and to a reprobate mind;' and to be *realizing in the madness of her pro-slavery career, the fulfillment of that awful declaration of the apostle,—'God shall send them strong delusions, that they might all be damned;*

because they obeyed not the truth but had pleasure in unrighteousness." Page 123.

Thus the reader sees that even the Doctors of the M. E. Church, who have waited and watched for years with earnest solicitude to behold any signs of returning health, have been compelled at last to abandon all hope of her ever recovering. A church thus hopelessly given up by her best and wiset friends, as being so wedded to the abominable sin of slavery that she cannot be reformed, surely cannot be the Church of God! A church "given over to a hardness of heart, and to a reprobate mind,"—a church "realizing *in the madness of her pro-slavery career*," the dreadful malediction pronounced by the apostle, "God shall send them strong delusions that they might all be damned," cannot possibly be the Church of God! God never thus deals with his genuine people. But he does thus deal with those who have become incorrigibly wicked." (See Thes. ii. 7, 13.) Think of it! A church upon whom God is sending strong delusions, that they might believe a lie!—that they might be damned—still claiming to be the Church of Christ! Can anything be more preposterous and absurd? And yet such is the character and condition of the M. E. Church before God this day, if Dr. BOWEN is to be believed. Then is it not plainly the duty of all in that church who love the Saviour, and who desire to obey his holy commandments, to withdraw from a church thus corrupted in her moral character, and thus abandoned and cursed of God? When is secession a duty, if not in this case?

———

One more Bible view of this subject and we are done. By comparing the present position of the M. E. Church on the subject of Slavery, as described by HOSMER, DE VINNE,

LONG, MATTISON, and BOWEN, with the account given us in the Book of Revelation, of "*The Mystery of Iniquity,*" the reader, no doubt will be struck with the remarkable similarity and sameness by which both pictures are distinguished. By "*Babylon the great the mother of harlots and abominations of the earth,*" spoken of in the 17th and 18th chapters of Revelation, all commentators agree that we are to understand a corrupt and fallen church professing at the same time to be the Church of God. True, these commentators tell us we are to see in the Roman Catholic Church the living representation of Babylon the great that John describes. But they also tell us that as she is called "THE MOTHER OF HARLOTS," all those Protestant Churches who copy after her example in any of those particular sins which constitute her corruption and prostitution, may be deservedly called her daughters. Babylon's corruptions, and those of the M. E. Church are alike in many particulars. Instance the following :

1. Babylon had become the habitation of Devils. Rev. xviii. 2.

Doctor BOWEN says : "The *Demon* of Slavery has at length become installed over us as the *Genius Loci* of our institutions and government ; AND ALL OUR ADMINISTRATIONS AND MOVEMENTS IN GENERAL ARE NOW SUBJECT TO THE DOMINEERING SURVEILLANCE OF THIS RUTHLESS DIVINITY." (Intro., page 4.) Surely that place must be the habitation of devils where the Genius Loci (the God of the place) is a demon.

2. Babylon had "become the hold of every foul spirit." Rev. xviii. 2. Dr. BOWEN says : "The M. E. Church practically endorses a despotism, the *vilest, the most cruel, and the most fiendish this side of hell.*" Page 142. Rev. J.

D. LONG says: Slavery "*has debauched the moral sentiment of the whole church.*" Page 31. The Black River Conference says: "Our *complicity with the vile abomination* places us in the most fearful attitude before *the God of holiness.*"

3. Babylon, because of her costly temple and popularity, "glorified herself as a queen, and lived deliciously." Rev. xviii. 18. Dr. BOWEN says of the M. E. Church: "Who wonders that a church that can cherish the blinding, corrupting, and damning sin of slavery in her bosom, should come to substitute her growing numbers, her multiplied and costly temples, and her popularity and influence for the genuine Scriptural evidence of evangelical piety." Page 146.

4. Babylon, the Mystery of Iniquity, was given over to believe a lie that she might be damned. (See 2 Thes. ii. 7–12.) Doctor BOWEN says: The M. E. Church "is realizing the fulfillment of [that awful declaration of the apostle, God shall send them strong delusions that they may believe a lie! that they all may be damned, because they obeyed not the truth, but had pleasure in unrighteousness." Page 123.

5. Babylon was guilty of the blood of the souls of men. Rev. xvii. 6, 18, 24. Rev. J. D. LONG says: "What a fearful history has the M. E. Church to read to the world! *A history written in the blood and tears of oppressed thousands.*" Pages 30, 31.

6. Babylon made merchandize of the bodies and souls of men. Rev. xviii. 13. Rev. H. MATTISON says: "We have now from ten to twenty thousand slave-holders in our church, *who own, raise, buy and sell slaves,* as suits their convenience and interest." Page 84. Doctor BOWEN says,

the M. E. Church "*is to all intents and purposes a pro-slavery church*." Page 52.

7. Of Babylon, it is said, "Babylon the great is fallen," in consequence of her corruption. Rev. xviii. 2. Rev. H. MATTISON says: "So far as this subject (of Slavery) is concerned, *the M. E. Church in America is a fallen church*." Page 109.

8. God's people were commanded to come out of Babylon because she had ceased to be the Church of God, in consequence of her corruption. Rev. xviii. 4. God's people who yet remain in the M. E. Church, are commanded to secede from her communion and fellowship because she has ceased to be the Church of God, and has become a daughter of Babylon the great, by copying her example of tyranny and corruption.

INFERENTIAL REMARKS.

The M. E. Church is either the Church of Christ, or she is not. If the facts alleged against her by Doctor Bowen that she has lost her spirituality and conscience through the love of gain; "that she is to all intents and purposes a pro-slavery church;" and by J. D. Long, that "the moral sentiment of the whole church has become debauched"— "that her history is written in the blood and tears of oppressed thousands;" and by H. Mattison, that "the M. E. Church in America is a fallen church;" and by Wm. Hosmer, that "her profession of Christianity avails her nothing, in view of the boundless robbery she has committed in her apostacy from the holy principles of human freedom;"—if notwithstanding this entire and complete corruption of the M. E. Church though her complicity with "the sum of all villainies," she is still to be regarded as the Church of God, then it is plain that those who are causing dissensions, divisions, and in many instances secessions from the M. E. Church by agitating the subject of Slavery in her bosom, are guilty of schism—a crime as plainly con- demned in the word of God as any other. (See 1 Cor. xii. 25. Roms. xvi. 17.) It will not relieve the case of these schismatics to say that Slavery is an intruder in the M. E. Church, because this statement is not true. Slavery was in the M. E. Church from the beginning. Dr. Bowen tells us that "this dreadful cancer was upon the face ecclesiastic at our first organization." (Page 123.) Genuine anti- slavery principles and measures are, however, the real in- truders in the M. E. Church, and are therefore the primary cause of divisions in the church; and those who press such principles and measures are consequently schismatics. This is true if the M. E. Church is the Church of God.

On the other hand, if the M. E. Church, in consequence of her corrupt relation to "the sum of all villainies," has ceased to be the Church of Christ, as I have, I think abundantly shown to be the true state of the case, then the anti-slavery men, who are still in the M. E. Church, are committing sin by remaining there. (See following Scriptures: 2 Cor. vi. 14–18. 2 John x. and Rev. xviii. 4. Taking which horn of the dilema they may, Anti-slavery men in the M. E. Church are either guilty of schism, or of disobeying the Gospel doctrine of secession from the rank of God's enemies.

Reader, farewell! "Have no fellowship with the un fruitful works of darkness."